BEST FRIENDS FUR-EVER

WRITTEN AND ILLUSTRATED BY

Ruth McNally Barshaw

BLOOMSBURY

NEW YORK BERLIN LONDON SYDNEY

To Melanie and Erin and everyone who helped
make this book better

First published in the United States of America in August 2010
by Bloomsbury Books for Young Readers
Paperback edition published in July 2011
www.bloomsburykids.com

For information about permission to reproduce selections from this book, write to
Permissions, Bloomsbury BFYR, 175 Fifth Avenue, New York, New York 10010

The Library of Congress has cataloged the hardcover edition as follows:
Barshaw, Ruth McNally.
Ellie McDoodle : best friends fur-ever / by Ruth McNally Barshaw. — 1st U.S. ed.
p.   cm.
Summary: Ellie pet-sits for her neighbor's African grey parrot Alix, about whom she is writing
a report, while her family argues over whether to get a cat or a dog, and her little brother accidentally
lets Alix out of his cage, all of which is chronicled in Ellie's ever-present sketchbook.
ISBN 978-1-59990-426-9 (hardcover)
[1. Pets—Fiction. 2. African grey parrot—Fiction. 3. Parrots—Fiction. 4. Family life—Fiction.
5. Schools—Fiction. 6.Drawing—Fiction.] I. Title.
PZ7.B28047Elb 2010   [Fic]—dc22   2009046899

ISBN 978-1-59990-657-7 (paperback)

Typeset in Casino Hand
Art created with a Sanford Uni-ball Micro pen
Book design by Yelena Safronova

Printed in the U.S.A. by Quad/Graphics, Fairfield, Pennsylvania
1 3 5 7 9 10 8 6 4 2

All papers used by Bloomsbury Publishing, Inc., are natural, recyclable products made from wood grown in well-managed
forests. The manufacturing processes conform to the environmental regulations of the country of origin.

I hear them giggling. My older brother and sister are pranking me right this minute, right outside my door. I don't know what they're doing yet, but I do know this:

1) They will think it's hilarious.
2) I will not.

Josh and Risa are best friends, and I am their favorite victim. No worries—I get back at them whenever I can. I listen a while. Eventually, I sneak over and throw the door open wide to surprise them. But the joke's on me. The doorway is completely bricked in!

Cheezers.

Is that . . . a wrinkle?

Close inspection shows it's not real brick; it's just that sticky-back wallpaper people use to decorate or hide ugly things. Or whole rooms, like mine. Very convincing. This took some effort.

I sneak downstairs to catch them laughing about it, but they're already on to other things.

It's Ben-Ben Ball. Josh and Dad invented this weird mix of basketball, football, and dodgeball.

Ben-Ben is the ball. He's passed back and forth for five volleys, then he runs to the couch for a touchdown, six points. If he's intercepted by Dad and dunked into the laundry basket, Dad scores two points. Josh scores on assists with extra points if Ben-Ben touches the ceiling and penalty points if Mom sees them and gets mad.

Dad offers me a spot on the team:

We'll change the rules and call it Bellie Ball!

Er, no thank you.

Things at my house are so random and strange. Lately my family has been obsessed with pets.

Risa wants a cat because they're fun and adorable.

Mom wants no cats because she says they're horrible.

Josh votes for a dog.

Dad seconds it.

Mom says we aren't voting.

I say I'm happy with Ophelia. We don't need any more pets. (And if we had more, would Ophelia be safe?)

Risa says Ophelia could play with the cat.

Mom says there isn't any cat.

Josh says he wants a cat catapult.

Ben-Ben brings in his new pet pinecone.

Mom says that's exactly the right pet for us, then picks up a box and retreats to the kitchen. We moved to this house a while ago, but Mom is still unpacking.

Loud classical music composed by Paco Bell or someone like that.

Josh's buddies Izzy and Doof are here for band practice. Their opinion on a pet? A dog. Or a ferret.

This one's named DoggishCat. Izzy holds it out for me to pet. It's adorable. Until . . .

No ferrets.

the Tarantula Puppies ← Josh's band.
Josh says boys like tough or funny band names
and girls like cute names, so this one appeals to
both. He's planning to be famous.

band groupies   Risa's boyfriend, Peter

They're really good. Strange lyrics, though.

Puppy-puppy-puppy-puppy
Puppy-puppy-puppy-puppy
Old dog—My dog—DoggishCat—Why dog
This is just another song
'Bout why I'm right and you are wrong . . .

I watch. I don't try to make sense of it. Suddenly
Josh stops playing to announce that he thought of
an idea for a band T-shirt. He wants me to draw it.
(Hmm, maybe.) He runs upstairs to get it from his
room. And that's when we hear the scream.

I'm laughing so hard my stomach hurts. Risa's laughing so hard she's wiping her eyes. Everyone else looks totally freaked out, so we explain our weird family ritual.

Who she is: The evil Mrs. Claus from Mom's stash of Santa statues.

What we do: Hide Mrs. Claus to surprise each other.

Why we do it: Because she's evil and it's funny to creep each other out.

Best appearance so far: They're all good. That's the beauty of Mrs. Claus—when you least expect her, she appears, nightmare in hand.

Josh is so shaken he looks like he's going to throw up.

And just in time for dinner!

Mom wants a nice dinner with classical music, but we're all on pet overload.

I want a cat.

I don't want a mere cat. I want a meerkat. Did you know they make good hunter pets?

Nooo! No more Santas!

YES Santas! With real presents!

I agree. But Mom's an interior designer, obviously not a poet.

In school Mrs. Whittam assigns a huge project: Choose an animal. Study it for two weeks. Do a multimedia presentation in front of the class. No common domestic animals—no hamsters, dogs, cats, or rats. No repeats—if one student claims an animal for his or her project, nobody else can choose that animal. Some kids are actually excited about this.

I hate giving presentations. Can't I just turn in lots of art about my animal and forget the part about standing in front of the class, scared stiff and getting hives?

Me in second grade:

turning bright red →

← hives on neck

Class laughing. I didn't say anything funny.

Mrs. Johnson and Mom thought I had hives because of the orange juice I had for breakfast, so I wasn't allowed to have orange juice for three years. It wasn't a juice allergy. It's a class presentation allergy and I STILL HAVE IT.

I can see it now. I'll stand up in front of Mrs. Whittam's class with all my wretched hives and they'll think I'm a freak. I'll lose every friend I've made so far.

In fact, just thinking about it makes me feel a little itchy. I scratch. It's getting worse. I feel big bumps sprouting on my neck. They're very itchy. Does anyone else notice my hives? I can feel them! They're huge! ARGH! I can't stop scratching! The more I scratch, the more I want to scratch! Am I sick? My stomach hurts.

Everyone else knows what animal they want to study. All I can think of is that class presentation. Mo is so practical.

Llamas! The university llama festival is next weekend. I'll do all my research there.

Travis wants some sort of nasty predator, maybe a lamprey. Did you know they bore circular holes in innocent fish and suck out their blood? *shudder*

Glenda wants the nine-banded armadillo. There are six subspecies. Armadillos grunt, squeal, buzz, and purr. She saw one in Florida, waddling in a campground. It was gray and about nine inches long. Armadillos eat mostly insects but they'll also eat eggs and carrion, which is dead, decaying animals.

1. Don't tell us your whole presentation now.
2. Can we please stop talking about this gross stuff at lunch?

Mo wants me to pick parrots because one of my neighbors has one (weird how everyone knows everything about everyone else in this town).

No thanks. I know nothing about parrots. Besides, all they do is:

Polly wants a cracker!
Awwk!

Now everyone's doing it. We walk into Mr. Brendall's class as parrots begging for treats. Awwk!

After school, Mo, Travis, and I bike to the
pet store.

Weird bike, weird name for it: recumbent.

The store is so crowded with kids from my
class that it looks like a field trip. We all have the
same idea—research an animal for tomorrow.

Too bad we can't claim hamsters. This one's funny. "To eat or not to eat, that is the question." I call him Hamlet.

Why are people afraid of spiders and snakes? Snakes don't bug me but spiders give me the creeps. One crawled up my leg once. Freaked me out. I was jumping and yelling. I'm not doing my report on them.

The mealworm: insignificant to some, yet critical to the survival of others. Even people eat them. I don't know what mealworms taste like, but maybe I'll try one sometime. Maybe. Not soon. And I'm not doing my report on them.

The Flight Crew

Kids are claiming the macaw, cockatiel, and umbrella cockatoo, probably because they're so exotic and colorful.

Macaw rocking back and forth on a twig swing. He reminds me of Ben-Ben, always in motion.

Hello, hello, hello.

Beautiful, colorful wasted food and gunk.

Hello, my name is Sammy.

Sammy! Come back here, Sammy!

↖ This little Senegal parrot calls to himself when I walk away.

These grey Timnehs are ignored. Is it because they're not colorful or noisy? Why do I get the feeling they're very smart? And how is it that dolphins look like geniuses but goldfish don't?

I take the long way home, stopping at the woods to see animals without a price tag.

This red-tailed hawk is eating a—what is that? Never mind. I don't want to know.

I push over a rock and find this salamander. Silent liquid black, he slips out of my hand.

Shhh! A deer! She's gamboling in a clearing. I see her for just a few seconds, and then she ducks between two trees and is gone from my sight. That was beautiful. She danced for me.

I could claim one of these woodsy creatures. Or something I saw at the pet store. But I want something really special—something that, when everyone sees it, will make them ignore me and my hives.

At home Josh is building a geodesic dome out of straws.

(Risa wants a cat and leaves little reminders everywhere.)

Josh wants an alpaca. Why an alpaca?
His reasons:
1. They spit.
2. They can be housetrained.
3. After you're tired of petting them or weaving their hair, you can eat them.
YIKES.

How to Build a Geodesic Dome

Equipment:

- 25 poles (tubes, straws, pretzel rods, pencils, toothpicks . . . all sorts of choices. Pick one.)
- Something to connect the poles (tape, glue, gumdrops, etc.).

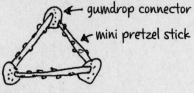

gumdrop connector

mini pretzel stick

1. Join 5 poles together with 5 connectors to make a pentagon.

Make sure all of the corners are well connected.

2. Add 2 connected poles upright to each bottom pole to form 5 triangles.

3. Connect the top of each triangle with a pole to make another pentagon.

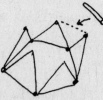

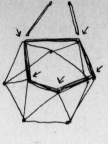

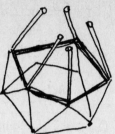

4. Connect 1 upright pole to each of the 5 corners.

5. Connect all the tips at the top, forming a star shape.

It's hard to draw but easy to make, especially with someone to help hold the poles.

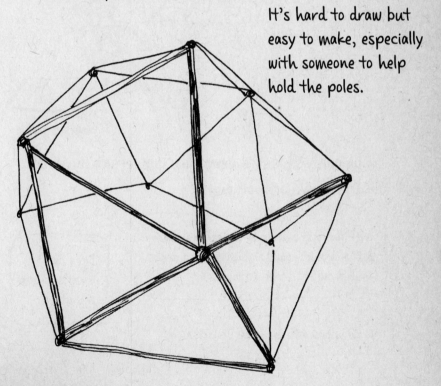

Dinner: We're talking in rhyme.
All of the time.

What's new in school?

Remember the rule.

I have to do a presentation but I have some reservations.

A new assignment from your teacher? Tell us what it has to feature.

pinecone picnic

Obviously this is a very slow conversation. What word rhymes with animal?

A thing that crawls or slides or walks.
A thing that roars or bleats or squawks.
And it can't . . . be a plant.

Do a cat. That's where it's at.

No dogs or cats. No mice or rats.

Pick a fly. They're pretty sly.

You should pick a horse, of course!

Know what I would really dig? If you did it on a pig.

You should pick a kangaroo. That one would be fun to do.

This is getting bad. Then we hear from Dad.

Please pass the beans. Pick a bird that preens.

I decree,
do a bee!

Study a finch—
good in a pinch!

Or a rhino with a horn.
Risa, please pass me the corn.

Pick something that's strange, like you.
To your own self be true.

Yeah! Pick a cod because you're odd.

Hey! That's not a nice thing to say!

And besides, it's not fair play.

So, lots of animals in rhyme.
Which of them is worth my time?

Ring!

Interruption, thank goodness. A phone call for me! It's Mrs. Morrow, who lives down the street. She wants me to birdsit her African Grey, Alix. She puts Alix on the phone to say hello.

Hello!

♡ ♡ ♡ ♡ ♡

Oh my gosh, I'm in love! How adorable! I can't wait to meet Alix tomorrow. Now Josh wants a parrot for a pet. He says, "Make Alix love you more than Mrs. Morrow, so he can live here." (And he didn't say it in rhyme.)

As I climb into bed I'm thinking I can combine the birdsitting job with my school project. Maybe I can teach Alix to say a few words. Then I see two glowing eyes . . .

I fall out of bed yelling. Eventually I calm down enough to figure it out. Josh and Risa tricked out Mrs. Claus by putting LED lights in her eye sockets. It's frightening (especially in the dark).

Do I hear giggling on the steps? Yep.

On safety patrol at the kindergarten doors the next morning, Glenda is talking nonstop about armadillos.

Armadillos spend most of their lives asleep.

Armadillos love to swim—and they're good at it.

Armadillos can't see very well. If you stay still, they might not notice you.

I like the little armor-plated rats as much as anyone does, but I'm tired of hearing about them!

I make up a fact about parrots.

I say, "African Grey parrots fly backward in the wild to confuse predators."

Glenda stares at me as if I'M flying backward, then says I should meet her uncle Conyer, a bird expert at the university and zoo. I say only if he'll give my presentation for me.

(no hives)

In Mrs. Whittam's class, we claim our animals by raising our hands and giving a fact about the animal we want to study. It's like tossing a tuna sandwich into a flock of seagulls—total feeding frenzy.

The popular animals go fast, and sometimes one kid claims an animal another kid wanted.

Fact: Kangaroos can jump twenty-five feet. Kangaroo claimed.

Fact: Bald eagles have a seven-foot wingspan. Bald eagle claimed.

Fact: Polar bears have black skin under their white fur. Polar bear claimed.

Fact: Duck-billed platypuses are mammals that lay eggs. Duck-billed platypus claimed.

I get the African Grey parrot. What a relief!

Yay!

But Kiera claims llamas before Mo can. Quickly, I slip one of Josh's alpaca facts to her.

pssst!

Mo claims alpacas.

Now Mo's excited about her project. I'm still worried about everyone seeing my grand hives display.

Lunchtime.

detention

straw wrapper

Glenda takes a swig of milk
at exactly the wrong time.

The spray reaches record
distances in all directions.

Ewww! Anyone have
spare napkins?

loop-de-loop

Everyone cheers. Ryan
bows. So all I have to do for my
presentation is shock, surprise,
entertain, and make a big splash.
Then the audience will cheer.
Maybe I can get Alix to perform
some flying stunts, too.

Renisha's soup. Ick!

After school I finally get to meet Alix!

Mrs. Morrow has a bird care to-do list for me.

- ☐ New food each morning (snacks and veggies).
- ☐ Fresh water.

- ☐ Line bottom of cage with yesterday's newspaper.
- ☐ Let Alix out of his cage for three hours every afternoon to play on his perch.
- ☐ Give him treats when he does something good.
- ☐ Visit Alix three times a day.
- ☐ Swap out toys every other day to prevent boredom.
- ☐ Keep him indoors always.
- ☐ Call if I have any problems or questions.

I have my own list:

- ☐ Make him love me.
- ☐ Teach him flying stunts.
- ☐ Teach him to tell some funny jokes.

I wish I could put a leash on him and fly him outside like a kite. That would be so cool. I would attach the leash to my belt loop and take him everywhere.

walking home from the art store

waiting outside school for me →

We'd win a kite-flying contest.

Wow, that kite looks like a real bird!

Alix and I are going to be best friends.

I ask if Alix can do any tricks. He can! Mrs. Morrow whistles one of Mom's classical tunes and Alix bobs and sways to the music. He catches treats in the air. He dances the "Hokey Pokey."

And he makes noises! He mimics the doorbell

Ding-dong.

and the telephone

Ring ring ringgg.

and even Mrs. Morrow!

Alix's tricks are cute, but I need to figure out what I can use for my project. I ask Mrs. Morrow if it's hard to teach Alix new phrases. She says sometimes, but other times he picks up something new after hearing it just once. We talk about my school project. I ask if we can bring Alix in to show the class. She says YES.

At home Risa says instead of
a cat she now wants a kitten.
Josh wants a Pekingese.
Or some peeking geese. Or
some Peking fleas.
Risa says, "It's not Peking,
it's Beijing. Jeez!" Then she
scrounges up dinner: "Have
some stinking cheese."
Josh says we can't have
a cat because he's allergic
to them. He blasts Risa with
a leaky sneeze. Risa says that
was fake so we should all
ignore Josh's geeky pleas.
I'm in awe, watching them
go back and forth. I can think
of rhyming words—tweaky,
cheeky, keys, peas—but I have
trouble making them work. Typical.
Every time I think I'm catching
up to Josh and Risa, they leap
away from me, whether it's
word games or running games.

Dad keeps it going. He says he's worried about creaking knees.

Mom says she's tired of teen music—shrieking banshees—and she changes the radio station to her Paco Bell music.

I tell them about Alix and his "speaking ease." Ben-Ben wants to go with me to visit Alix tomorrow. "Sure," I say generously. I'll share Alix.

pinecone kennel

While doing the dishes I notice some birds in the backyard. Two cardinals call to each other. The male is bright red. You can see him anywhere. The female is brown—the only pretty part is her orange beak. It's funny how boy birds are so beautiful to impress the girls, but girl birds don't worry about how they look. In people it's usually the opposite. Girls try to impress boys, and boys don't care how they look.

I'm watching the brown cardinal. She flies to the telephone wire and chirps. She may not be flashy, but she has something to say. This gives me a brilliant idea: maybe I can train Alix to recite my presentation points! Anything he can't manage I will put on posters. I won't have to speak at all! No hives!

Things I Want Alix to Say:

1. Polly wants a cracker, but Alix wants to talk to you about African Grey parrots. African Greys are Timnehs or Congos.

2. I am a Timneh. Wild Timnehs live in the rain forest and savannas of west-central Africa.

3. Timnehs have been pets for more than 4,000 years. You'll find them in hieroglyphics of ancient Egypt. King Henry VIII of England had one.

4. Unfortunately, the Timneh population is declining. Too many wild Timnehs are being captured and sold as pets.

5. Timnehs talk, but they also think about what they're saying.

6. Timnehs attach to one person. I'm attached to Ellie.

This is kind of dry stuff. I should spice it up. Risa says Peter's a hot piece of awesome. I don't know what that means, but it definitely sounds better than just saying Peter's cool.

7. Ellie is a brilliant piece of awesome.

I visit Alix in the morning. Mrs. Morrow doesn't leave for vacation until tomorrow, but she wants me to have alone time with Alix, so she goes outside. Alix and I get right down to business. I read all of my presentation points out loud, making sure to speak clearly. I tell him to repeat what I said. He doesn't.

I don't have much time. I have to get his food and water and then I have to go to school. I try just the first line of my presentation: "Polly wants a cracker, but Alix wants to talk to you about African Grey parrots."

He won't repeat it. Maybe it's too long to start with. I say, "Polly wants a cracker, but Alix wants to talk." No luck.

I say, "Ellie is a brilliant piece of awesome." Alix says, "Good-bye." Whoa. He can't mean that. Maybe he knows I'll be late for school if I don't run now. Smart bird. More later.

In Mrs. Whittam's class, more kids claim animals.

Travis: Mike the Wonder Chicken lived eighteen months without a head. Chicken now claimed. Everyone laughs like crazy.

Ryan: The bird-dropping moth uses camouflage to hide right out in the open. Everyone laughs hysterically.

Mrs. Whittam is very still. She narrows her eyes, raises an eyebrow, and stares hard at Ryan.

I can tell he's trying hard not to smirk. Everyone gets quiet.

Mrs. Whittam challenges Ryan to prove this is a real animal, and he only has five minutes. Ryan walks to the classroom computer and types in a few words. Everyone watches. Who will win this showdown?

beads of sweat?

Finally Mrs. Whittam calls all of us up to view the Internet page on the screen. It's a big picture of a moth that looks amazingly like a bird dropping. Everyone is high-fiving Ryan and saying how cool it is. Even Mrs. Whittam is grinning.

wing

head

leg

antenna

The claiming continues.

Dong claims the black widow spider. Fact: A spider's silk is strong and stretchy. He holds up a sample.

Wow.

Mackenzie claims Chihuahuas. Fact: They have the largest brain of any dog for their size. But Mrs. Whittam says no dogs. Gage says no rats, and no rat-dogs. Everyone laughs except Mackenzie.

Aww!

Mason claims the water moccasin. Fact: It's a snake, not a shoe.

Eek!!

Isaac claims a new bird species, the Nonggang babbler. Mrs. Whittam challenges him: is there enough info available to do a full report?

Huh?

Isaac starts spouting facts: it was recently found in China near Vietnam; it runs more than it flies . . . Mrs. Whittam stops him. Babbler claimed!

Alyssa picks the monarch butterfly. Fact: Michigan monarchs migrate to Michoacan, Mexico. Mrs. Whittam gives her an extra point for alliteration, with all those m's.

Gage picks the Komodo dragon. Fact: They bite their prey, infecting it with bacteria, and come back for it later when it's dead. All the boys cheer.

I notice that the boys claim either funny or scary animals. Why is this?

Is a male butterfly less male than a male Komodo dragon? Butterflies have to work hard to get out of a chrysalis and start flying. I've seen them. It's not a job for lightweights. So why don't they get the same respect as tough-guy animals?

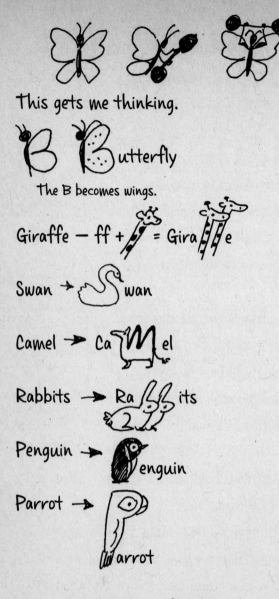

This gets me thinking.

B Butterfly

The B becomes wings.

Giraffe — ff + = Gira e

Swan → Swan

Camel → Ca M el

Rabbits → Ra its

Penguin → enguin

Parrot → arrot

My name! Ellie McDOOdle.

I just invented Ellie McDoodle Words.

Step 1: Write a word on your paper.

Example: **Tree**

Step 2: Take out a letter and replace it with an image that explains the word.

Flowers . . .

I show them to my afternoon teacher (science, math, and geography), Mr. Brendall. He says I could use this for part of my animal project. Good idea!

After school I go to Mrs. Morrow's house with Ben-Ben. Alix is super attentive to Ben-Ben. His whole body turns to watch as Ben-Ben races around the room. Mrs. Morrow says she's never seen anything like it.

She's so excited that she gets Ben-Ben some treats to feed to Alix.

Then she gets more treats—for Ben-Ben to eat. Like he needs more energy!

It's a lovefest. Actually, it's kind of annoying to watch, and I'm stuck here for two more hours so Alix can get enough perch time.

I wish I'd brought some homework to do.

Ben-Ben jumps. Alix bounces.

Ben-Ben whoops. Alix repeats.

Ben-Ben giggles. Alix cackles. (I roll my eyes.)

Alix makes a doorbell sound. Ben-Ben laughs and says "Ding-dong!"

Alix fluffs up his feathers and flaps his wings. Ben-Ben waves his arms and shakes his tail feathers in a little dance.

Alix makes a smoochy sound. Ben-Ben blows kisses.

Mrs. Morrow is elated. Mrs. Morrow ♡s this. I ♡ this. Next time I'm not bringing Ben-Ben.

I'm stuck. I don't want to be here. I might as well do something useful. I brainstorm for my project.

Other things I can do:
  - diorama
  - papier-mâché flying bird model
  - origami animal
  ⭐ a game! Achi: tic-tac-toe on steroids

ACHI

This game comes from Ghana. Kids draw the game board in the dirt and use stones for markers.

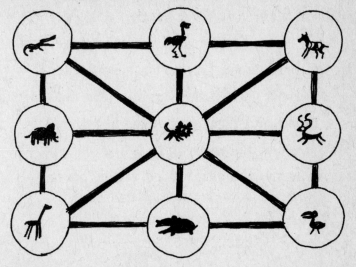

TO PLAY: Two players. Each player has four markers (coins, bottle caps, checkers, whatever).

TO WIN: Line up three of your markers in a row vertically, horizontally, or diagonally.

DROP: Each player in turn puts one of their four markers on an empty circle. Be careful—don't let the other player put three in a row!

MOVE: When all of the markers are on the board, players take turns sliding one of their markers along any line to an empty circle, until a row of three markers is formed. The first player to line up three markers in a row wins.

Back at home, Risa says she used to want a kitten, but now she will compromise for any one of the following: kitten, kitty, feline, tomcat, tabby, or cat. Fact: House cats kill millions of songbirds each year. Dad wants a dog.

Fact: Some dog breeds were specifically bred to rid the world of rats. I don't want various links of the food chain living here and treating Ophelia like dinner.

It's a weird day when Josh is the voice of reason. He says no cat, no dog. I ♡ily agree.

Let's get a racing cow!

Um, Josh? You feeling okay? ("Voice of reason"?)

Fact: The cows at the university have number cards connected to their ears, I guess so the researchers can keep track of them. Josh calls them racing cows. A racing turtle makes as much sense to me.

Mom wants her under-the-counter CD player installed. Risa volunteers. Strange . . . Risa hardly ever does something nice without expecting something in return.

I have a question for the group: "How do you get someone to like you more?"

Josh: "Kidnap them, put them in a tower, and never let them see another human."

Okay, that's creepy.
Risa: "Let them do a favor for you."
I say, "Hmm, Risa has gotten me to do a zillion favors for her, yet I don't like her more."

And then things get ugly.

Risa asks if this is about a boy I like. I say NO, but she gives me the googly eyes and starts batting her eyelashes. She says, "Start wearing lipstick and pretty clothes."

Eww. If a guy liked me better just for that, I don't think he'd be the kind of guy I would like. WHAT AM I THINKING?! I tell her this is NOT, repeat, NOT about a boy.

Josh says to be strategic: "Figure out what he likes, and do that."

Risa says, "And wear perfume!"

Dad says, "Be a team player and make him cookies. That's how I won your mom."

(Then he and Mom kiss. Eww.)

Risa says, "Vanilla perfume!"

Josh says, "Make us a batch of cookies, spill some ingredients on yourself, and forget the perfume."

Risa says, "That's a crumby idea." Get it? Crumbs.

Mom says to be myself, and if a boy doesn't like me the way I am then he isn't worth liking. Moms are supposed to say that sort of thing.

They're having so much fun with this that I don't have the ♡ to tell them it's NOT ABOUT A BOY. It's about a bird. Cheezers.

How do I get Alix to like me? Rub birdseed perfume on my arms? Act like Ben-Ben? Do African Greys like monkey boys because they both live in the Congo?

Is it puppy love?

Monkey love?

I visit Alix again after Ben-Ben is in bed. I bring treats and try my phrases on Alix. No luck. I think it'll be easier once Mrs. Morrow is away and I can really concentrate.

I . . . am . . . a . . . Tim-neh.

talking super slow

Tomorrow will be my first day alone with Alix. As I am leaving, Mrs. Morrow makes me promise to bring Ben-Ben over a few times to see Alix since they get along so well. Yippee.

Before going to bed, I train Ophelia to dance in a circle for a treat. Okay, this looks less like dancing and more like a dog chasing its tail, but this proves I am good at training animals. So why am I having so much trouble with Alix?

I should get Ophelia to deliver my presentation instead of Alix. Problem: she can't talk. Can I teach her sign language in time? No.

I love you, Ophelia.

I know—maybe Alix will learn better if I bring Ophelia over and demonstrate how it's done. I'll train her in front of him and he'll want to learn!

In school, Mr. Brendall has us take apart owl pellets. He says it's an example of the kind of creativity that's expected with our projects.

stuffed barn owl from museum

owl pellet, actual size

It smells like dirt. It's black and brown with bits of white showing. Also some dark fuzz. It's smooth, mostly, and lightweight. It looks like a big dirt egg. Travis rigs up this sort of scale. One owl pellet weighs about the same as one glue stick. Hmm.

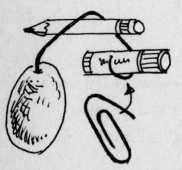

We dig through the owl pellets. It's like archaeology: we're digging for bones. The fuzz is undigested fur.

Eww.

The bones are from birds and rodents. The owl eats the animal, and the parts it can't digest get compacted together to form a pellet that it spits out. It's totally gross and totally fascinating at the same time. We have charts to glue our treasures onto:

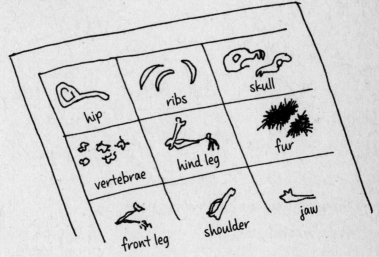

My owl pellet has three complete skulls of mice or rats. It's horrifying to see proof that some birds eat rodents. Alix is a big bird. Ophelia is a rather small rodent. Maybe it's a bad idea for them to meet.

Ryan's making one of his little skulls "eat" things. Gross.

After school I get ready to head to Alix's. Dad asks me how it's going. I tell him I'm tackling the impossible. He mentions the Hail Mary pass.

Huh?

He asks how much I really want this.

Huh, again?

Dad launches into one of his sports metaphors. "It's the end of the game. Your team's losing by five. It's third down and twelve yards to the goal line. Do you try for the first down, or do you try for a touchdown? You can play it safe, but you won't gain as much. If you try hard for a bigger goal, a lot of times you get what you want."

Okay. I think I understand: make a big play and try for the impossible. "Thanks, Dad."

But wait. There's more.

"On the other hand," Dad says, "sometimes it's better to try for small goals. If you have time, go for the few yards to get the next down and make it easier to next try for a touchdown. Progress toward the goal is steady and incremental."

Er, okay . . .

Next he throws in a tortoise-and-hare thing: slow and steady wins the race.

"Dad, this is a fumble. Stick to one idea at a time?"

Josh comes in. He's eating a cucumber wrapped in a banana peel. What in the—?

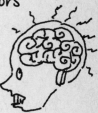

He says, "How do you eat an elephant? One small bite at a time."

I think my brain's about to explode with all the sports and animal metaphors fighting for attention. I grab control. "This is my challenge and I'm going to handle it my way."

Take the bull by the horns!

Don't put the cart before the horse!

Grab the tiger by the tail!

You draw more flies with honey!

Cheezers. I'm trying. I'm in it to win it. I'm both the tortoise AND the hare. Plus the bull, the horse, and the tiger. Okay, maybe not. But I can definitely draw flies.

"Alix, say: 'Ellie is a brilliant piece of awesome.'"

Ellie is a silly-greasy-awful!

Alix didn't really say that.
I didn't hear him right, did I?

Ellie is a silly-greasy-awful!

He's playing. He's in a playful mood. I should
get him some toys and treats from the pet store.
That will make him want to say the right words
for me.

Go on now. Get going.

Snubbed by a bird.

Maybe parrots aren't as smart
as I thought they were.

75

This kid is watching
everything I do.

Why is everything
so expensive?

Oops, did I say that
out loud?

All I want to do is buy some stupid treats and
get that stupid bird to do my stupid presentation.
I move to the next aisle. The kid follows. He has
a name tag. He works here! He gets paid to
annoy people?

Spy Guy offers to help. I say I need parrot treats for training, but I guess it comes out sounding kind of crabby. I can't help it! I'm in a bad mood! He scowls and asks what I'm trying to get the bird to do. I say I'm trying to get the birdbrain I'm birdsitting to do my evil bidding and help me take over the world. It's sarcasm, which this "Marc" kid doesn't understand. He starts a lecture about how birds are highly intelligent and a good judge of people, and if this bird doesn't like me there might be a good reason. I don't need his rude-dude attitude! I grab a random bag of treats and walk fast to the checkout line.

Alix likes the treat. The only thing I can get him to say is "Polly wants a cracker." And, of course, "Ellie is a silly-greasy-awful." I'm about to give up when Risa comes in with Ben-Ben.

Alix watches Ben-Ben. Ben-Ben watches Alix. I watch them both. Which means nobody watches Risa. She flips through my cue cards of words for Alix to say. And then she says the most damaging thing possible, the thing that will ring in my ears forever . . .

"Ellie, you are CRAZYpants!"

Of course, Alix repeats it instantly. Of course, Risa and Ben-Ben laugh hysterically. Of course, Alix says it again. And again. And AGAIN. How do you un-teach a bird? Is it possible? How do you make sure he doesn't say it during your presentation in front of the class?

More hives.

I start packing up my stuff without saying a word. May as well go home. There's nothing to do here. Everything I say can and will be used against me by that stinking bird and my rotten sister and that pesky little monkey boy.

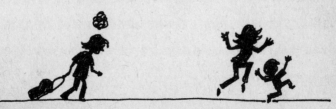

Josh asks Puppetypup, his sock puppet, how he knows I am crazypants.

Risa says even Alix says I am.

Great. Now I'm being harrassed by a bird AND a sock puppet. Thank goodness Ben-Ben never talks. I'm not sure I could handle more of this. I drag my backpack upstairs to work on my animal project in peace.

I'm going to win this. I spend the next hour recording my presentation. I'll play it a zillion times for Alix and he'll get it right. But since he hasn't been very cooperative, I'll make sure the rest of my presentation is extra great. Just in case.

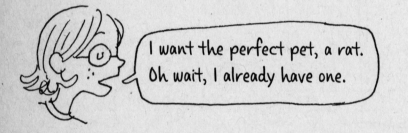

Breakfast: Josh wants to get an albino rhinoceros. An albino rhino. Josh doesn't say these things just for laughs. I think I've figured out his strategy: by asking Mom for weird pets, he is more likely to get what he really wants— a dog.

> I want the perfect pet, a rat. Oh wait, I already have one.

Ben-Ben gives each of us a pet pinecone. Mom brings out some stuff to decorate them. Josh's does tricks already.

> Roll over! Good boy!

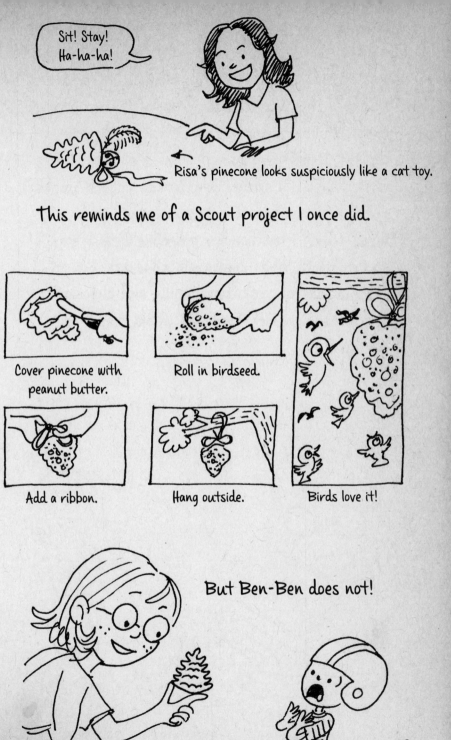

Sit! Stay! Ha-ha-ha!

Risa's pinecone looks suspiciously like a cat toy.

This reminds me of a Scout project I once did.

Cover pinecone with peanut butter.

Roll in birdseed.

Add a ribbon.

Hang outside.

Birds love it!

But Ben-Ben does not!

Ben-Ben thinks I'm going to make my pet pinecone into a birdfeeder. I promise him I won't—cross my heart, hope to die, stick a pinecone in my eye. Ben-Ben does not think I'm funny but Josh smirks. "I swear, Ben-Ben, I will NOT make my dear sweet adorable pet pinecone into a birdfeeder." I position my pinecone with treats all around it. What does a pinecone eat? I'm thinking cereal, cinnamon candy, and chocolate sprinkles. Ben-Ben approves. Mom rolls her eyes.

All this pinecone stuff has made me late. At Mrs. Morrow's house I set up my voice recording for an infinite loop. Alix will hear the whole hour seven times while I'm at school and he'll be ready for the next step when I get back. I'm a genius.

In school Mrs. Whittam reminds us we have one week until our projects are due. She says it's a huge part of our grade and we should be using every resource possible. Plus we have to list where we get our facts and it can't be a Web site. I predict a mad rush for the library after school.

Work hard!
Play hard!

Play hard? Yes. Mr. Brendall says when you work extra hard, you should take time out to refill your creative brain. So we share animal jokes:

What do you call a fish with no eyes? A fsh.
What do you call a deer with no eyes? No eye-deer!
What's a porcupine's favorite dance? The "Hokey Pokey."
Why are fish always in schools? Because they don't like
    to play hooky.
Why was the cat afraid to climb a tree? Because of its bark.
What do you give a seasick elephant? Lots of room.

A bunch of us go to the library to check out books about our animals. Miss Claire helps—I tell her about Alix and she loads me down with a ton of books.

book about a
famous parrot
↓

training your parrot

African birds

wild parrots →

bird crafts

flight

bird brains

Perfect! It's a lot to carry home but now I have everything I need. My plan is to finish my project this weekend. I have three days, there's nothing going on at my house, and I can work at Alix's house if I need more space. This will be easy! I'm almost excited.

I drop everything while walking into my house because . . . Oh. My. Gosh. No way—

WE HAVE A NEW PUPPY!

Dad says his friend at work can't keep it because of her allergies. Her loss is our HUGE gain. The puppy is adorable. Dad says we have to pull together 110% (like that's possible) to take good care of it (I volunteer) and everything is on the line (uh, now this is about football?) so let's all step up to the plate (wait, that's baseball?).

Attempted translation: Dad wanted a dog more than Mom did, so let's help her to like it.

The puppy lets us pet him. Pretty soon he warms up to us and he jumps and licks our faces, ears, eyes (eww). When he runs, he sort of leads with his right shoulder, almost running sideways. It's so cute!

Josh and I have a contest: we both call the puppy and see who he runs to most. It's an even split. He likes us both.

Bad news: the puppy piddles on the floor. Does Mom freak out? No, but she makes us promise to handle every part of taking care of him—training, vet visits, cleanup, exercise. No problem! I'm first to take him for a walk.

thrilled   ecstatic   sort of calm (why?)

giggling nonstop

With those fat little legs, Fargo and I don't go very far.

My chosen name doesn't last very long. Josh says we're calling him Mr. Manly Tough Brute Grizzly Guy! Er . . . right. We'll see about that. I'm off to visit Mr. Feathery Stubborn Guy.

The puppy ♥s me. Alix 🔺s me. He keeps making sounds to fool me.

I run to answer the phone—but it's not ringing. Alix is ringing.

I run to answer the doorbell—but there's nobody there. It's Alix.

I hear the computer magically turn on. I run to see how. It's just start-up noises. Alix again.

The microwave buzzes and beeps. You guessed it.

Alix is driving me crazy, and the worst part is he knows it. He laughs at me! He's cackling!

Plus he won't learn the cue cards for my presentation. He is obstreperous, obstinate, and obnoxious! Those are my three best words—but I don't tell him, because with my luck he'll repeat them to Mrs. Morrow.

I have to remember my goal. The trick is to make Alix want to help me.

Okay, deep breaths. Patience. Try again. I start with the basics: a treat in my hand and one word, "Hello."

"Hello, Alix. Hello."

Hello.

I give him a treat. Good boy. We repeat it three times, three treats. Perfect! We move to the next cue card: Polly wants a cracker. He won't say it. He says Alix wants a cracker.

Argh!

Deep breaths. I can do this. Back to the beginning.

encouraging smile

I say:	Alix answers:
Hello, hello, hello.	Hello, hello, hello.

Treat, treat, treat.

| Polly wants a cracker. | Alix wants a cracker. |

Okay, fine. We can rewrite the cue cards.

| Hello. | Hello. |

Treat.

| My name is Alix. | My name is Alix. |

Treat.

| Let's talk about African Grey parrots. | No. |

No treat.

Alix is upside down, licking his toenails.

What a pain! Why can't he just cooperate?
I'm in Mrs. Morrow's kitchen, looking up
parrot-training Web sites on their computer,
when he starts making sound effects again.

pussy
willow

Ding-dong!

"Stop it, Alix."

Ding-dong!

"Alix, cut it out. I'm not falling for that."

Ding-dong!
Ding-dong!

Oh. It really is the doorbell. Worse: it's
Ben-Ben.

Great. Alix has a pet name for Ben-Ben. How adorable. How utterly fantastic—not! Alix won't repeat words for a very important school project but he'll do anything for Ben-Ben.

Hey . . . maybe I can get Ben-Ben to help me teach Alix what to do.

This could work. With Ben-Ben giving the treats, maybe Alix will cooperate more. It's worth a try.

Just then the phone rings (for real). It's Mrs. Morrow! She sounds happy when I say Ben-Ben is here for a visit, and she laughs at his new Whoosh-Whoosh nickname. Alix and Ben-Ben are so loud that I take the phone into the kitchen, where I can hear better.

I don't tell her how useless Alix has been. I say I'm in control and everything's fine. I ask for some Alix facts. Mrs. Morrow says he's ten years old. He likes seeds, nuts, bread, chicken, veggies, fruit, and rice stuffed into toilet paper tubes (yum). I tell her I'm trying to teach Alix to say something new and she says he already knows hundreds of words! We talk a while, and then I go check on Alix and Ben-Ben.

Oh my GOSH! Ben-Ben and Alix are making a mess of the living room. This is terrible!

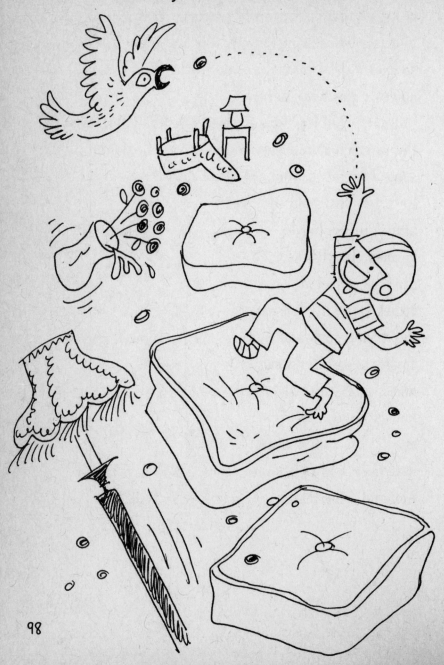

I tell Ben-Ben to stop, but he's making so much noise he can't hear me. A lamp crashes.

"Stop! Get out! Now!"

For a second Ben-Ben freezes. Then he runs out the front door—and before I can rush over to close it, Alix swoops outside after him!

I try to catch Ben-Ben first. I didn't mean to scare him.

No! Wait! Don't cry!

Alix is circling overhead, screeching.

I'm sorry. Don't cry. It's okay. See, you're fine.

I carry Ben-Ben home while keeping an eye on Alix the whole time (and hoping I don't trip and fall). I shove Ben-Ben into the house (gently but fast!), telling him to play with the new puppy. Then I chase after Alix.

Alix is on Mrs. Morrow's roof. I try every phrase he likes. I get his favorite treats. I extend a broom up toward him so he can climb on it and I can lower him back down to me. He looks at me and walks to the back side of the roof.

I run to the backyard and call him. I beg him to come down. Nothing works. And then . . . he flies off!

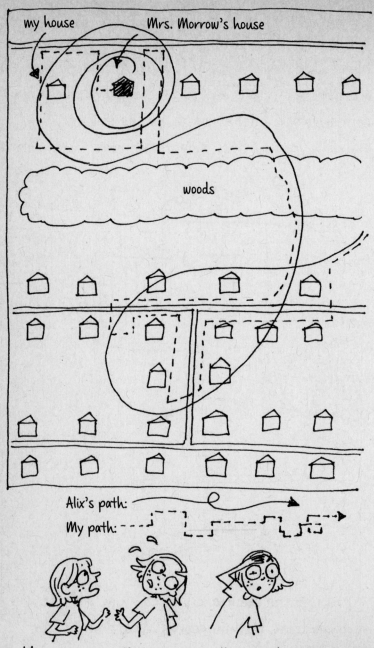

This is crazy. I'm running all over the place.

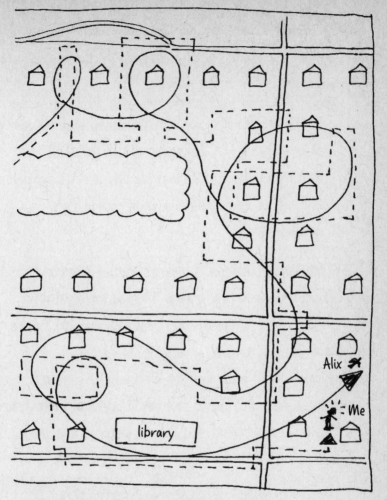

I lose sight of Alix outside the library. Now what? Maybe Miss Claire will know what to do. I rush inside and tell her the whole awful story—even though it's embarrassing. What kind of pet sitter loses the pet?

Miss Claire hands me a thick book and tells me to look up "lost parrot" in the index. The book says:

- Don't let your bird escape. (Um, too late.)
- Lost pet parrots can live successfully on their own—a flock of 1,200 lives in Los Angeles!
- Put an ad about your lost bird in the newspaper and online. (And tell the whole world he's missing? No.)

This book is useless. I look for more parrot books, but there aren't any. Then I remember why—I checked them all out! All the parrot books are back at my house.

I'm looking for help on the Web when Glenda comes over. Uh-oh! She's the LAST person I want to see. If she hears about Alix, she'll blab to everyone.

I'm out of here. Good-bye, armadillo girl.

Walking home, I watch the sky. Where's Alix? Maybe he's waiting for me on Mrs. Morrow's porch! This thought makes me run.

But Alix isn't there. I see about thirty crows, some Canada geese flying south for the winter, a red cardinal, and some cute little birds with V-shaped tails. They dive and swoop in big loopy circles, like they're having a party.

Alix will come back, won't he? Is he just having fun flying with the other birds?

I sit on the porch a while and then I go home.
I'm late for dinner but on time to do the
dishes. I've decided I'm not going to tell my family
about Alix yet. Ben-Ben doesn't talk, so he won't
tell them either. Risa and Josh are installing Mom's
CD player. Correction: they're TRYING to. It isn't
going very well. They've drilled a lot of extra
holes and they're
starting to swear.

Normally this
would be huge
entertainment, but
I have to watch the window. Maybe Alix will fly
by and I'll coax him into Mrs. Morrow's house
and nobody will ever know he got loose.

Ben-Ben comes into the kitchen. I know what he's thinking. I whisper, "No, I didn't catch Alix yet." He looks at me with the biggest, saddest eyes I've ever seen in my whole life. Then he picks up the pet pinecone he gave me earlier and leaves. I know what this means: he blames me for losing Alix and he thinks I'm terrible at taking care of pets.

Ben-Ben, wait. Do you want me to read you a story?

He keeps walking. Ben-Ben, who loves stories and is always bouncy like a balloon, walks like he has my heavy backpack tied to his ankles. He trudges upstairs, goes to his room, and shuts the door. My eyes water.

I finish the dishes and go outside to look for Alix. I see Josh walking our sweet puppy. They play a bit and then go inside our house. They don't notice me watching from Mrs. Morrow's porch. Babysitting an empty house is lonely and boring. I'd rather do anything else—even homework.

I move to the backyard. The trees cast spooky shadows. The stars are out. Ursa Minor, Camelopardalis, Pegasus, Cygnus—funny how many constellations are named for animals. Silent fireflies glitter around me like stars fallen to earth. I wish they could give me a bright idea on how to bring Alix back.

Eventually I give up and come home and read all the parrot books cover to cover. They don't tell me anything new.

I was going to make Alix a star at my school.
And he was going to help me give a no-hives
presentation.

That rotten Ben-Ben wrecked everything. I
want to throttle him! But I sort of already did by
yelling at him. I can't swallow. My throat hurts.

What am I going to do? Should I call Mrs.
Morrow? No. I have to get Alix back by myself.

My dreams are no better than real life.

Today is Saturday. No school. I want to play with our new puppy all morning but Mom reminds me that it's my job to take care of Alix so I go to Alix's house. (If she only knew!)

I am staring at Alix's empty cage when suddenly I get an idea.

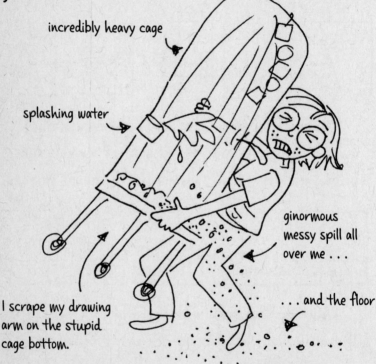

incredibly heavy cage

splashing water

ginormous messy spill all over me . . .

. . . and the floor

I scrape my drawing arm on the stupid cage bottom.

I finally get the cage out to the backyard. I'm hoping Alix will see it and fly in. (Note to self: next time empty the food and water dishes BEFORE moving the cage. Argh.)

I sit outside with the empty birdcage for two hours.

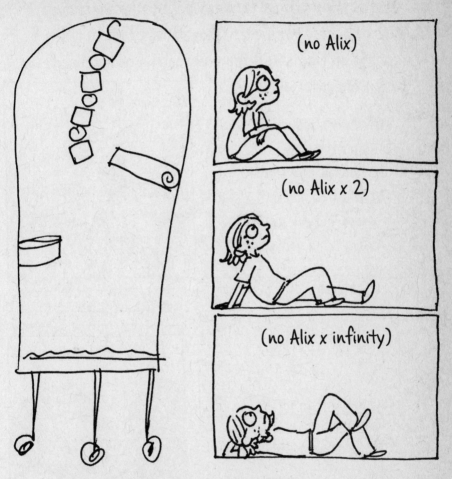

(no Alix)

(no Alix x 2)

(no Alix x infinity)

Then I haul it back inside and clean up the mess I made earlier. The vacuum cleaner doesn't pick up birdseed very well. What a nightmare. I have to get out of here.

When I get home there's a message for me: Mo and Travis want me to meet them at the zoo. Mom's okay with it because we'll be researching our projects. I've never been to this zoo, so when I get there Travis and Mo give me the grand tour, complete with jokes.

Q: What's a shark's favorite game?
A: Swallow the leader.
Q: What do you call a shark wearing ear muffs?
A: Anything you want.

snowy owl

He looks very talon-ted.

bull shark

ring-tailed lemurs

These poor zombies need names:
Die-ann of the Dead Sea.
Livvy of Lake Eerie.
Ghouldilocks!
They're three ghoulfriends.

Q: What's their favorite game?
A: Hide-and-shriek.

The Siberian tiger looks at us like we're lunch.

Q: Why do tigers have stripes?

A: So they won't be spotted.

Laughing, we name him Spot.

twitching tail

Q: What do you get when you cross a porcupine with a turtle?

A: A slow poke.

tortoise

50 years old

scarlet macaw

Q: What did the geometry teacher say when she lost her parrot?

A: Where's my polygon?

YIKES. Suddenly I remember Alix, and I feel sick. Mo asks what's wrong, so I tell them about his escape. Of course, they're horrified. (This does NOT make me feel better.)

But they do have an idea I wouldn't have thought of: Glenda's uncle Conyer is the bird expert here at the zoo. They go to research their projects. I go to find Uncle Conyer. Bird expert? He's a bird himself!

crest

beady eyes

duck tail

sharp beak

squawky voice

jittery, nervous, always looking around (for worms?)

long, skinny flamingo legs

long, sharp toenails?

(He thinks I'm taking notes. I won't let him see this page. Incriminating!)

I tell him I've got some questions about parrots and he interrupts, telling me about a famous African Grey parrot who proved that birds are smart. Then he gets so jumpy I expect feathers to start flying. He's all over the office, pulling books off shelves and articles out of folders and photos out of envelopes to show me. He's talking so fast I don't get a chance to tell him about my problem with Alix! Suddenly he gets a phone call. Two minutes later he's flying out of the office saying he has a bird fossil discovery to investigate, and he's pushing me down the hall through a door . . .

Before I know it I'm watching a "Birds of Prey" show. Uncle Conyer said I should speak to the bird guy afterward if I have any questions about parrots. Waaait . . . this guy looks familiar.

Marc

He's the pet store kid! Cheezers! I don't care how much he knows, I'm NOT talking to him.

I bail out. I'd rather see the rest of the zoo.

The Penguinarium

This is awesome. The room is circular and we stand in the middle, so it's like being in the exhibit with the penguins. I wish I could climb through the glass and slide, dive, and waddle with them. Not sure I'd like the diet—all raw fish, all the time. They're playing on ice, so it must be super cold in the water. Weird that these penguins are from the south. I keep thinking only the north is cold.

I wish I'd picked penguins for my project. These would make great cartoon characters.

I start playing with the idea of penguins as comic strip characters:

Picky Penguin, the Rockhopper Penguin. She hops. Looks grouchy. Is she a teacher? Sister? Mean bully at school?

Nice kid character, like me. Ha! Is this a younger sister? Main character?

I'm thinking about the penguins and what it's like to be one, or to own one as a pet, and I'm brainstorming penguin comics, and walking, not paying attention to what's around me, when—

OOF!

I crash into someone. Well, not someone—it's
the rude dude from the pet store and the show.
How embarrassing! Two pens go flying. Two books
fall. His looks like a journal too. He snatches up
MY journal and when he notices the sketches he
starts flipping through pages. I try to grab it
back but he's holding it over his head. Grr!

I can't believe this! The rude guy has MY BOOK and I can't get it back. I'm saying, "GIVE ME MY BOOK," and he's saying, "Just a minute, hold on." It's maddening. I notice his book, pick it up, and run to the other side of the Penguinarium to read it. Two can play this game! And this is the crazy part . . .

He draws comics. Some of them are actually funny. It's a bit shocking—he's an artist like I am? He isn't just a rude creep in a pet store? Who knew? I didn't—my brain can't adjust to this.

Suddenly he's behind me. He hands me my book and his pen. He says my pen broke so I can keep his. Then he says he likes my art. He's smiling. I don't know what to say. This doesn't fit together—he's being nice? To me?

He does this hand motion and says, "Awkward turtle!"

Ha-ha. So the kid can make a turtle with his hands. I want to respond in a smart way, but it comes out of my mouth as a guffaw, like a shout-laugh, which is embarrassing.

To distract him from it, I tell him some of his comics are funny. He's still smiling. I can feel my face going red so I just point to a page and say this one's pretty good (which it is).

It's crazy that I'm standing here talking about comics with my enemy. Okay, maybe enemy is too strong a word. Foe, rival, bane of my existence?

He talks fast, but what surprises me is that I'm interested in what he says. We compare sketches of his parents' pet store, and we've both drawn the same animals!

I hear a loud growl and it makes me laugh—it's his stomach. Now it's his turn to go red in the face. He wants to go to the Snack Attack Shack because they make good smoothies. We do, and that's where we invent Smoothie Comics:

You're such
a knife guy.

muffin

English muffin

'Ello, bloke!

Pretzel drama:
No, Rod, stay away from her. She's
twisted!

I scream.

You do have a point there.

Cheezers!

I'm nachos anymore!

We crack ourselves up.
Maybe this Marc guy isn't so bad.

Mo and Travis find us. I introduce them to Marc. We all want to see more of the zoo.

Travis: "Check out that unusual wildlife."

Mo: "That's called a gaggle of geese."

Me: "Chased by a gaggle of girls."

Marc: "More like a giggle of girls!"

Travis: "If a group of geese is called a gaggle, what's a group of gags called? A geesle?"

Er-wow! Er-wow! A very pretty peacock shows off. Marc says I can't call it pretty because it's a male—it's undignified. We're having so much fun! I don't want it to end.

We pass the camels, and Mo asks if I've ever ridden one.

Turns out it's a rocky-rolly ride, a completely different feel than a horse. Plus I'm incredibly high up. Please, camel, do not run.

Thank you so much, Mo, for taking a photo of me looking terrified.

My legs are doing the splits.

While walking (well, I am waddling) to our bikes, I find a ♡ rock.

Mo and I make plans to go to LlamaRama tomorrow. Marc says he'll be there, too, working at his family's booth. I say, "Maybe I'll bump into you there!" and he says, "I'll wear my crash helmet." I laugh, and it comes out like a pig snort. I turn red, and everyone laughs at me.

I laugh at me, too.

When I get home it's back to reality. I haul all of my project stuff over to Alix's house to work there. I have to find Alix, and soon!

Marc's pen

I drag all my parrot-attracting props outside.

But the cage doesn't bring Alix home. Nothing does. I drag it all back inside and go home.

Josh is training the puppy.

Ben-Ben seems to have formed a special bond with him.

We eat dinner by candlelight—that is, the lights are all off except for Ben-Ben's fireflies. Mom's not-yet-installed CD player provides dinner music: Paco Bell, Yo-Hands-Trouse, and Bay-toe-ven. Er, Beethoven. We discuss some puppy names. Rex, Buddy, Max, Fido. Fido? Really, Josh?

Mom says we should name the puppy after someone smart and hope it rubs off on him. Josh says we can't, because the name Josh is already taken. After groaning, more suggestions: Copernicus, Galileo Galilei, Sir Francis Bacon, Shakespeare, Henry Wadsworth Longfellow.

"That's it," Mom says. Henry Wadsworth Longfellow is his name? I guess it fits. He's long. Josh says it's only fair that Mom gets to name him since Henry will be more trouble for her than for any of us. Mom glares at Josh while we all giggle.

After dinner I go back to Alix's house to keep up my bird-watching act. There's nothing worse than watching an empty cage. When I get tired of working on my project, I list all of my ideas for catching an escaped pet.

Already tried these:

call to it
throw treats to it
make cage seem inviting
lure it with toys
look for help in books

Can't do these:

hire a professional
alert the neighbors
newspaper ad
make lost pet posters
set a trap

Cheezers. Now what?

Before bed, Mom tells me how proud of me she is for taking such good care of Alix. Luckily my mouth is full of toothpaste so I can only say, "Mmffmgf!"

So I'm in bed and can't sleep. Maybe a snack will help? I hear scratching on Risa's door—is the puppy in there? I open her door and SOMETHING runs out. It's dark in the hall, but whatever that was, it was NOT a puppy.

WHAT IS THAT?!
A TARANTULA?

Risa runs out, too, and dashes downstairs. I follow behind at a safe distance. If that's a giant spider, I don't want it running up my leg.

Whatever it is, Risa scoops it up and PUTS IT INSIDE HER BATHROBE!!! And she says I'M crazypants?

I whisper-yell, "Is that a tarantula?"

Risa whisper-yells back, "Shh! It's nothing, you llabfoog.* Go to bed!"

Weird how she can make me feel like an insignificant little idiot. I'm not letting go of this, though. I beg, "Please tell me. Please, please, please, please, please, please, please!" And probably to shut me up, she finally says okay.

*llabfoog = goofball backward

Oh. My. GOSH.
It's a kitten!
Does Mom know?
Where'd you get it?
Are you insane?
Mom's going to kill you.
Oh my gosh.
Mom won't let you
keep it, will she?
Can I hold it?

She's adorable!
Risa's boyfriend gave
it to her. She's been
hiding in Risa's room
for a week!
   I promise not to tell
anyone. Mostly because I
think Mom's going to go
ballistic and I don't want
to be around for that.

I'm up early in the morning to play secretly with Risa's fun-size cat. She's super cute, but she scratches me! On my drawing arm! She has big feet—extra toes . . . which mean extra claws. Owww! Risa is not sympathetic.

The cat claws me, Henry has sharp puppy teeth, and Alix says rude things. Ophelia is in absolutely no danger of losing favored pet status with me!

At breakfast Mom tells me again how proud of me she is for looking after Alix. My mouth is full of cereal so I say, "Mmffmgf." Mom says Mrs. Morrow should pay me extra.

Mo's picking me up to go to LlamaRama in a few hours, so I go over to "check on Alix" and wait. I'm sick of working on my project and I'm sick of looking for that rotten bird. He must have flown back to the African Congo by now.

I make an origami penguin because it reminds me of the zoo:

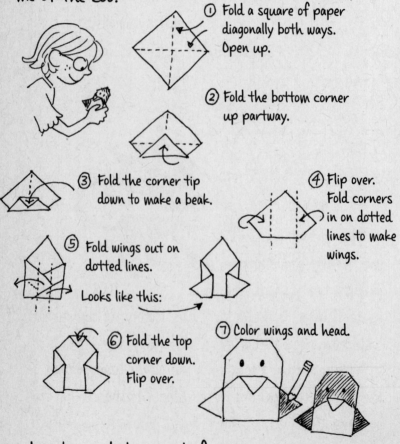

① Fold a square of paper diagonally both ways. Open up.

② Fold the bottom corner up partway.

③ Fold the corner tip down to make a beak.

④ Flip over. Fold corners in on dotted lines to make wings.

⑤ Fold wings out on dotted lines.

Looks like this:

⑥ Fold the top corner down. Flip over.

⑦ Color wings and head.

I make a whole passel of penguins.

Mo's family finally arrives to take me to LlamaRama. I'm really excited to go—plus I am SO ready to leave Mrs. Morrow's house with its empty birdcage. Before we go, Mo's brother, Thomas, has to play with Henry.

Thomas has Down syndrome, which means he has trouble learning—but I learn things from him all the time! I just treat him like a friend and say nice things to him.

Watching Thomas with Henry is funny. Thomas is giggling because the puppy's licking his face, and that makes all of us laugh.

Diana, Mo's sister

We're at LlamaRama, the huge llama and alpaca show at the university livestock pavilion.

Wow. There are llamas and alpacas EVERYWHERE being washed, combed, sheared, petted, fed, paraded, and judged.

Fact: Someone crossed a puppy with a pony and that's how we got llamas and alpacas. Okay, NOT true. I made that up.

How to Draw a Llama:

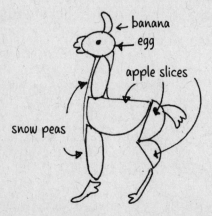

← banana
← egg
apple slices
snow peas

We're surrounded by strange sounds, sights, and especially smells. There's lots to do. We point out our favorite llamas and we talk with the owners. Mo asks a lot of questions for her alpaca project. I get to weave some alpaca fiber into a blanket; it's so soft and pretty.

Mo and I hear some girls doing a llama song with hand motions, but we can't hear all the words and we're too chicken 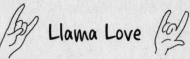 to ask. So we make up our own.

Llama Love

Happy llama

Up for drama

Says good-bye

To his mama

Turns into a

Super llama

Flying to the

LlamaRama!

But Super Llama

Misses Mama

It's too much llama

Melodrama!

Says good-bye

To LlamaRama

Flies home to

His mama llama.

>kiss<

We practice it about fifty times until we memorize it.

We're doing our llama song when we see Marc
at his store's booth. I ask why boys hardly ever do
goofy hand motion songs. Marc shrugs and says,
"I do." Right then, an alpaca makes a clucking
noise next to his cheek. Marc
says, "Aww, thanks,
sweetie pie." I
guffaw, as usual.

We check out
Marc's booth.
They have all
kinds of stuff for and about animals: books,
leashes, toys, clothes—and a mini zoo, including a
few parrots. This gives me an idea: maybe I'll buy
a new Alix. I quietly ask Marc's dad how much an
African Grey parrot costs.

He says, "Fourteen ninety-five."

Just $14.95? I can definitely afford that!

Then he says, "Fourteen HUNDRED ninety-
five dollars."

Oh. Well. Um. Yeah. I gotta go catch up with
Marc and Mo . . .

On the way home, Mo and I teach Diana our llama song. If she teaches it to her friends, and they teach it to all their

friends, maybe kids all over the world will catch on and Mo and I will become famous. That would be EPIC.

Diana and Thomas want to play with Henry again, so I take Mo up to my room to hang out. Suddenly we hear loud barking coming from outside. We scramble to the window, afraid that something's wrong. And it is!

All the neighbors are gathered on my lawn watching the puppy, who's barking furiously at . . .

Risa's CAT! This is going to be good. We run out there as fast as we can.

Rark! Rark!

Hisssssssss!

twitchy tail like the zoo tiger

The neighbors start to bet on who'll win (odds are definitely in the cat's favor).

The puppy's just playing, but unfortunately the cat is serious!

Mmrairr!

Yipe yipe yipe!

I notice Mom giving Risa the stink eye. Whoa. Looks like she just found out about the cat! Lucky for Risa, Josh interrupts with comic relief: "What does a dyslexic dog say? Krab! Krab! Fur! Fur!" Everyone groans. Then Josh announces his band will be performing their first concert here after dinner. I don't get to see how Risa and Mom handle the cat because they go inside. (Too bad, no fireworks.)

At night the Tarantula Puppies perform.
Everyone in the neighborhood comes. It's rockin'!

Some of my school friends—cool!

Risa and Peter. Eeeewwww!

Mo, Travis, and
I set up front row
seats, complete with
snacks. It's kind of chilly

grapes to throw (hee hee)

out here. Which makes me wonder: how long can
a rainforest parrot live in the cold?

Later, when I'm getting ready for bed, I look in the mirror and see a weasel. Nice one, Josh.

Ben-Ben leaves a message on my pillow:

his drawing of Alix surrounded by my heart rock collection

He misses Alix.

Ben-Ben doesn't know how hard I've been trying to find Alix. I am putting a lot of thought into this! But feeding Ophelia makes me think:

what if SHE were lost? I would be worried sick.

Alix, this is my solemn pledge: I will redouble my efforts. I MUST bring you home safe.

I get reminded of my pledge at breakfast.

"Ellie, darling, I know you've had a lot to do lately and chores have interfered. I have good news for you: Risa's being punished for sneaking in the cat. She has to do the dishes for the next two years, which means you'll have more time for your school project and taking care of Alix!"

Yippee. More hours with the empty cage.

On the way to school I see a crow. I swear it's laughing at me. Aren't crows traditionally a hint of bad things to come? What more bad stuff could come?

CAW, CAW!

At school, Mrs. Whittam asks if anyone is ready to give a presentation—and two kids volunteer! How could anyone be that organized this early? This is deeply disturbing. But I get something good out of Cinda's demonstration.

How to Make a Leopard Puppet:

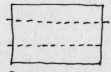

① Divide a sheet of paper into thirds

② Fold sides in on dotted lines

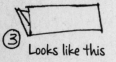

③ Looks like this

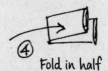

④ Fold in half

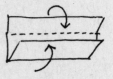

⑤ Fold top back

⑥ Fold bottom back

⑦ Looks like a zigzag

⑧ Draw and decorate the face—tape on ears, tongue, etc.

⑨ Fingers go in top opening, thumb goes in bottom opening.

Mr. Brendall gives us time to work on our animal projects. Mine needs a lot more work, but I can't concentrate on it. I get an hour on the class computer and this is what I type:

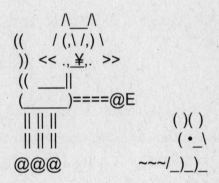

```
           /\__/\
  ((    / (,\ / /,) \
   ))  << .,_¥,. >>
  ((   ___||
  (_____)====@E
   || || ||              ( )( )
   || || ||              ( •_\
  @@@                  ~~~/_)_)_
```

It's an evil cat with big toes and really big claws, swiping at a cute little mouse.

I wonder if Alix is in danger from any cats. We have hawks in the woods behind our house. "Do hawks eat parrots?" I ask Mo after school. She doesn't know. She suggests I call Marc for help, but what would he think of me? I can't call him. Not until I'm desperate—and there has to be something I can still do.

After school at Alix's I get creative.

Plan A: Giant pile of bird food.

It attracts a huge crowd of the wrong kind of bird. Ugh. And when a large number of birds eat a large amount of food, there's a very disgusting result. It takes a long time to completely hose down the yard.

Plan B: Yelling Alix words into a megaphone borrowed from Dad's coaching equipment.

Megaphones are LOUD. It's embarrassing telling the neighborhood I am silly, greasy, awful, AND crazypants. But I do. And yet it does no good. Still no sign of Alix.

Plan C: I play Mrs. Morrow's answering machine voice over the megaphone too.

"Hello, we're not able to come to the phone right now, but please leave a message after the beep . . ."

Plan D: An Alix kite.

two cardboard strips

white plastic bag with a parrot drawn on it

I fly my Alix kite as high as I can. I'm thinking, Of course, this will bring Alix home! It doesn't. Nothing does. It's dinnertime. I'll have to try again later.

Walking into my house (MY OWN HOUSE), I am ambushed by Risa's adorable little skin shredder. You can't pull her off. She's clingy and clawful.

Meow!

Yeow!

She is razor teeth plus fur. Snookums Scissorhands.

After dinner I race back to Alix's house and try everything all over again. I'm incredibly productive. I'm amazingly creative. I'm alarmingly unsuccessful. No Alix.

I am calling the cat "First
Aid Kit" from now on.

What That Evil Cat's Claws Are Good For:

- converting curtains to vertical blinds
- untangling spaghetti
- raking sand in a mini Zen garden
- slicing onions
- creating confetti

- dividing cake into five equal parts (er, six, no,
  seven, depending on which foot she uses)
- getting that frayed look on your jeans,
  T-shirts, coats, legs . . .

I didn't sleep well last night. I couldn't stop thinking about Alix. Maybe he's mad at me and doesn't want to be found. Or, worse, what if something happened to him?

I go to Alix's house for my morning routine, even though I know it's probably a waste of time—and it is. Then I walk to school, watching the sky the whole way. I keep thinking I hear Alix, but it's just my imagination.

In Mrs. Whittam's class, Anna does her presentation on buffalo. Er, bison. We learn it's bison. Buffalo are in Asia and Africa.

Shawn tells us about donkeys and he even brings in a donkey piñata for us to whack. Free candy! That is SO awesome! This cheers me up.

As soon as I get home from school, Mom makes us all go to the vet. "It's to give Henry a healthy start with us," she says. Good, but we're also bringing Risa's Dread Cat, which means we're keeping her. I ♥ the cat.

The vet's waiting room is filled with every dog breed imaginable. Plus some cats, a duck, and a pig.

crabby grabby tabby

Henry is crazy-happy to be here.

Dr. Phillips calls us in. Our evil cat  follows, which panics Henry, who

barrels through the exam room into the hallway, followed by the , who frightens a Great Dane , who is slipping and sliding on the waxed floor, and we're all scrambling to catch a leash or a collar but trying desperately not to get scratched or bitten. It's chaos! And of course all the dogs in the kennel and the waiting room are going berserk, barking. Finally the vet opens a can of the stinkiest gunk I've ever smelled. The cat stops to eat the revolting roadkill-in-a-can , and I almost feel sorry for her because she believes it's actually food. All the animals are shoved into separate rooms . . .

152

And you can hear the collective sigh of relief.

Dr. Phillips examines Henry. He says he's healthy, gives him a shot, and trims his toenails. He says Henry will grow to forty pounds. Mom almost faints. She'd prefer a purse dog, I think.

When my family starts to leave, I hang back and spill it fast: "How do I get Alix back?" (This is my big reason for coming.)

Dr. Phillips says that birds form attachments, so Alix might come back for something or someone he loves. He says I should ask the owner—and I should hurry because there are predators in the area, it's a valuable bird, and the nights can get cold. Okay, fine.

Things Alix truly loves:

- making telephone ringing noises
- making fun of me
- fruit
- Mrs. Morrow
- Ben-Ben
- singing opera
- being read to
- swinging on his hammock
- _____?
- (not me) :(

Weird how car fronts look like faces.

eye   mouth   eye

154

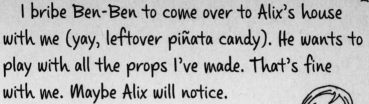

I bribe Ben-Ben to come over to Alix's house with me (yay, leftover piñata candy). He wants to play with all the props I've made. That's fine with me. Maybe Alix will notice.

Result: No Alix.

Breakfast:

I decide to do a good deed.

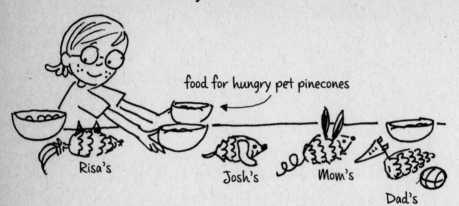

food for hungry pet pinecones

Risa's   Josh's   Mom's   Dad's

At Alix's house I move his cage and food to the
back door. I'm thinking positive: I'm getting him to
come home today. I should have the cage ready.

Mr. Good Luck, I'm ready for you to visit me.
I'm ready for Alix to return. Really, really ready.

At school, I ask Glenda how her armadillo project is coming along. We compare notes. See, I am being nice. Don't I deserve to have Alix return?

At lunch, Rachel asks me how my research with Alix is going. I look her in the eye and say, "Well, he likes Ben-Ben best. And lately he's been kind of distant." Mo almost gags on her milk.

Travis interrupts. "When little birdies are knocked unconscious, what do they see?"

Walking home after school is painful. What have I done to find Alix? Obviously not enough. What should I have done? I probably should have called Mrs. Morrow the moment Alix got out.

What could I still do? Hmm. There isn't much left to try. I have a feeling he's up there, watching, and doesn't want to come home for me.

This is the longest, worst walk I've ever taken. By the time I get to my block, I know I don't really have a choice anymore. I have to do what's best for Alix.

When I get home, I walk straight to the
telephone and call Mrs. Morrow. My family
notices. Quietly they gather around me. It's
really cool—a silent, strong show of support—
while I find the words to tell Mrs. Morrow
that her beloved bird has been missing.

I can't believe it! Mrs. Morrow isn't angry.
She says this has happened before, even though
Alix's wings are clipped. She tells me what to
do and says she's coming home tomorrow, so no
matter what happens it'll be okay. Major relief
as I hang up.

And then the firestorm starts.

Risa: "Llabfoog—you should have told us Alix got loose! We'd have done something!"

Josh: "No man is an island, and no miss is an isthmus. You shouldn't try to do everything alone."

Mom: "Honey, you should have trusted us with your secret. What happens to one of us affects all of us."

Dad: "Teams work together. Aren't we a team?"

Whoa. I didn't realize it might actually be selfish to keep my problems to myself. I've been as stubborn as Terror Cat clinging to a leg.

After they're done scolding, they hug me and ask how they can help.

I make a list of supplies for everyone to get. Then I go upstairs for my binoculars, but mostly to breathe for a few minutes.

That was hard.

My long nightmare is ending.

I just breathe—yoga breathing that Risa taught me. A long breath in, hold it, long breath out.

Breathe. Breathe. Breathe. Breathe. Breathe.

Before going outside, I call Mo and tell her what happened, and ask her to call Travis and Marc and bring them to my house. If I can't get Alix back tonight, I at least want to be with my best friends.

Mom with a CD player playing Paco Bell. Er, Pachelbel. That's Alix's favorite song, too! It's super loud. Even louder because of Dad's megaphone.

Josh and Risa fall down laughing.

Alix is here! How to get him to come down to us? Think. Think like a bird . . . If I could fly I could go up there, grab him, and bring him down. Go up there . . . Aha! I climb the tallest tree in the yard (Mom's worried). I climb higher and higher. Looking down at my family, I realize what a good family they are. I'm glad they're mine! My little family. My teeny, tiny microscopic family. They sure seem small from up here! Ben-Ben in his helmet resembles a fast-moving chicken egg. Suddenly I get a BRILLIANT idea! I climb down fast and start to explain.

Mrs. Claus is here??

163

Miss Claire  stops by with a new parrot book for me. So I put her to work too! She helps Mom keep the Pachelbel music blaring. Dad sets out ladders and measures off a wide circle on the lawn. Mo , Travis , and Marc arrive just in time to be sent out for supplies. Josh and Risa call for more reinforcements: Doof , Izzy , and Peter .

staplers

red paper

white bedsheets

tons of newspapers

Working as fast as we can, we make dozens of newspaper rolls and staple them together. The plan: build a giant geodesic dome.

Meanwhile, Alix is perched high above us, reciting my presentation. "I am a Timneh. Wild Timnehs live in the rain forest and savannas of west-central Africa." Sigh. He knows my presentation! I don't know whether to give him a treat or scold him for not cooperating earlier!

With everyone's help we make a bunch of red-striped sheets and a tent-size geodesic dome. We put it all together, and . . .

This is SO awesome.

Ta-daaa! It looks like an oversized Ben-Ben helmet! Well, it doesn't look like one to us down here, but from up in the sky I bet it does. Sure enough, Alix comes swooping down, calling for Whoosh-Whoosh.

Ben-Ben makes a squawking noise and easily leads Alix into the cage. I call Mrs. Morrow on the spot and let Alix talk to her. And then we celebrate!

Pizza for everyone! Music courtesy of the Tarantula Puppies! Treats for Alix, who seems very happy to be home, thank goodness. Risa and Josh are working on a new trick: they're teaching Alix to call me a *schlub* but it doesn't even bug me. I'm so relieved to have found Alix!!!

Mom and Dad hug me and say they're proud of me. It feels good because this time I know I earned it.

Back at our house, the dog vs. cat craziness continues.

Bitey and Frighty

The cat and dog are like the rest of my family— usually underfoot, sometimes painful, definitely never boring. I can't watch them, though. I have to focus on finishing my project.

I thought of a new plan for the presentation. Each person in class gets a different BINGO scorecard (this is where a computer comes in handy).

As I mention a topic (for instance, McDoodle words, how feathers work, parrots as pets, parrot vocabulary, or funny things Alix does), kids cross off that square. The first to get five in a row yells "BINGO!" and wins the prize: a peanut butter pinecone birdfeeder (not one of Ben-Ben's pinecones, of course).

Each square is a topic from my presentation.

Today's the day. I'm ready to give my presentation, and I'm not bringing Alix in for it. I don't need him telling the whole school I'm crazypants.
I'm nervous and scared so I pack my lucky stuff:

Yay! Ben-Ben gives back my pinecone pet.

fake confidence

four-leaf clover

heart rock

Marc's pen

penny minted the year I was born

favorite shirt

Everyone has advice:
- Start with a joke!
- K.I.S.S.—Keep It Simple, Sweetie.
- Practice—let muscle memory bring victory!
- Be your own wonderful self.
- Doesn't say anything. He just runs, which means keep going, don't slow down.
- Hello, hello, hello! Have fun!

In class, my hand shoots up when Mrs. Whittam asks for a volunteer to give his or her presentation. At first I'm so jittery that my voice cracks, but I keep going. Eventually it's not so bad—I even like it a little, especially when the class laughs as I say something funny (I tell the polygon riddle).

I present a lot of facts about African Grey parrots but I also manage to tie in some of what I learned with Alix—like how birds in the wild work together for a common goal, just like good friends do. And how birds squawk to let others know when they need help—something I should have done a lot earlier. The bingo idea works great. Best part: no hives.

Mo and I decide to celebrate after school by going to Marc's store to buy some dog and cat treats. But first we have to check on Alix (I'll keep him INSIDE the cage this time). He'll razz me and call me crazypants, but that's okay. I can handle it.

The Ends
No animals were harmed in the making of this book.

Flip through the pages quickly to see a flying bird animation.

ACKNOWLEDGMENTS

Special thanks to this flock of helpers: Evan Rapin, Alyssa Forsthoefel, Abigail Cunningham, Jerald Bullock, Dave Brigham, Diane Allen, Nelson Phillips, Marty Smith, Dawn Dixon, Tim Bogar, Ann Finkelstein, Debbie Diesen, April Jo Young, Amy Huntley, Lori Van Hoesen, Kay Grimnes, Buffy Silverman, Toni Belanger, Charlie Barshaw, and Lisa, Joe, Katie, and Emily Barshaw.

Turn the page for exciting Ellie extras:

Learn to Draw Your Own Furry Friends

A sneak peek of Ellie's next adventure

Learn to Draw Your Own
Furry Friends

Risa's Cat

Start with a football head
and a banana body

Add legs and ears

Then toes and a tail

Give it a face

A Dog

Start with a square
and an apple slice

Add a snout and a face

Then an ear and legs

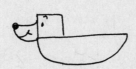

Finish with a tail and a collar

Try smoothing it out like this

A Zebra

Start with two triangles as the head and neck

Add ears and a snout

Trace a jawline

Add a nose and a neckline

Sketch a mane and a forelock

Add a line to the mane to make stripes

Finish with stripes on the body

Other animals you can make with this shape:

Donkey

Unicorn

Goat

A Squirrel

Start with a rounded triangle and a circle

Add ears and a face

Connect the pieces and add a foot

Add a mouselike tail and hand

Make the tail bushy and give it an acorn

Other animals you can make with this shape:

Bunny

Beaver

Skunk

A Dragon

Start with two triangles

Draw the curvy
top of the face

Finish the mouth and jawline
and use ovals for the body

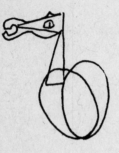

Add arms and feet

Round the neck and add
horns and wings

Add a tail and scales and
make it breathe fire

What's up next for Ellie McDoodle?

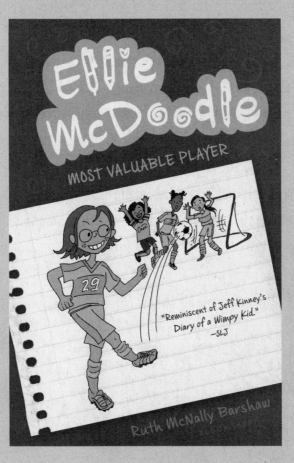

Read on for a sneak peek

BLOOMSBURY
www.bloomsburykids.com

Mo and I talk while packing up from Journey.

    Mo: I'm trying out for the parks and rec
         soccer team tomorrow. You should, too.

    Me: Soccer? I don't know ANYTHING about
         soccer! What if I stink?

    Mo: You won't. It's easy—just kick the ball into
         the goal. I'll help you.

    Me: Our Journey meetings will get in the way.

    Mo: The games and meetings are on different
         days. We can do both.

I lob objection after objection at Mo. She
returns each one without breaking a sweat.

    Finally, I'm out of excuses, so it's settled. We're
trying out for soccer tomorrow.

I'm so excited about soccer I can't wait to practice. I've seen soccer players heading the ball. As the star of the team, I'll need to be able to do that.

I invent my own drill:

1. Drop the ball on my head.

2. Watch which direction the ball bounces off my head.

3. Step on the ball with the foot furthest from the ball.

I drill myself over and over, fifty times in fifteen minutes.

I'll be the most valuable player, easy. With Mo and Dad on my side, I can't lose!

When I tell Dad I'm trying out for soccer, I expect him to pat me on the head and say I'll be the best player in the league. Instead, he drops this shocker: he's the new coach!

He's taking over for a coaching buddy who had to quit. Dad planned to ask ME to join the team!

Wait—DAD is my coach? Imagine the possibilities! He'll go easy on me. He'll practice with me. He'll be so proud of me he'll let me out of doing chores. This will be a cinch!

Me: Do I have to call you Coach McDougal?

Dad: No. You can call me Dad.

That night I have happy soccer dreams.

In the morning I can't wait to tell Mo the news about Dad being our coach. I kick the soccer ball all the way to school. (I admit, I'm showing off a little.)

By the time I get halfway to school my legs ache from keeping them stiff to kick.

I'm getting really good at this, though.

My on-the-way-to-school soccer practice is fantastic.

English class is going just fine.

And then the day takes a nasty turn . . .

Science stinks—literally!

Sitka's rubbing magazine perfume on her wrists. Jamian's secretly texting. Ahmed's snoring. I'm doing the work without their help.

I show my finished paper to Mr. Brendall.

Good news: I got all the answers right.

Bad news: we're also graded on how well our group worked together. A perfect score plus a terrible score equals a crummy score.

On the way home from school, I kick the soccer ball extra hard (which means I'm running a lot, because that ball goes sailing all over the place).

Soccer tryouts are held at the field by the high school. Everyone's from different schools.

Dad explains that he works at the university as a coach who coaches other coaches. He hasn't played much soccer, so we'll all learn together. I think I hear a few groans. This makes my protective instincts jump into overdrive. I scowl at the groaners.

It looks like we'll have a pretty strong team:

Danka   Hanna   Loni   Zoni

Boni   Toni   Joni   Roni   Sparkle-Sunshine

(I might have gotten some of the names wrong.)

These girls are amazing.

Victoria

Fifa

Mo

Um . . . this is just an off day

Everyone who tries out makes it onto the team. Dad gets Victoria to demonstrate how to kick the ball.

Instep: yes.   Side of foot: yes.   My way: no.

We'll have practice almost every day. That's a LOT of practice. I wonder if I'll get sick of soccer?

RUTH McNALLY BARSHAW, lifelong writer and artist, has worked in the advertising field, illustrated for newspapers, and won numerous essay-writing contests. She lives in Lansing, Michigan, with her family. Ruth is also the author of Ellie's other adventures, including her latest, *Ellie McDoodle: Most Valuable Player*. Visit her at www.ruthexpress.com.

We run laps, crab walk, and dance sideways, kicking balls. I fall six times. My legs are pretzels!

On the way home, Dad goes into hyper-energy mode, talking loud and fast about how talented the girls are and how many games we'll win. When I ask how he thinks I'm doing, he almost crashes into a construction barrel. He sputters, "Good work for your first day! Keep at it! You can do it!"

Hmm. He doesn't sound convinced. And I'm not sure I am, either.